Dedicated to all
Police Officers
and their families.

Be safe always.

TEN Police Officers get called to a crime...

One takes the criminal to jail,
and then there were **NINE**!

NINE Police Officers catch someone breaking into a closed gate...

One chases after him, and
then there were EIGHT!

EIGHT Police Officers taking

orders they are given...

One stays to write a
report, and then there
were SEVEN!

SEVEN Police Officers see a

flat tire they need to fix...

One helps the driver, and then
there were SIX!

SIX Police Officers going on a drive...

One makes a traffic stop, and
then there were FIVE!

FIVE Police Officers walk

through the station door...

One finishes her shift for the day,
and then there were **FOUR**!

FOUR Police Officers helping

people like you and me...

BLUE
One answers a call on the radio, and then there were THREE!

THREE Police Officers

looking after you...

One helps a woman cross the street,
and then there were TWO!

TWO Police Officers joining the local kids for some fun...

One stays to teach the students, and then there was ONE!

ONE Police Officer sitting all alone

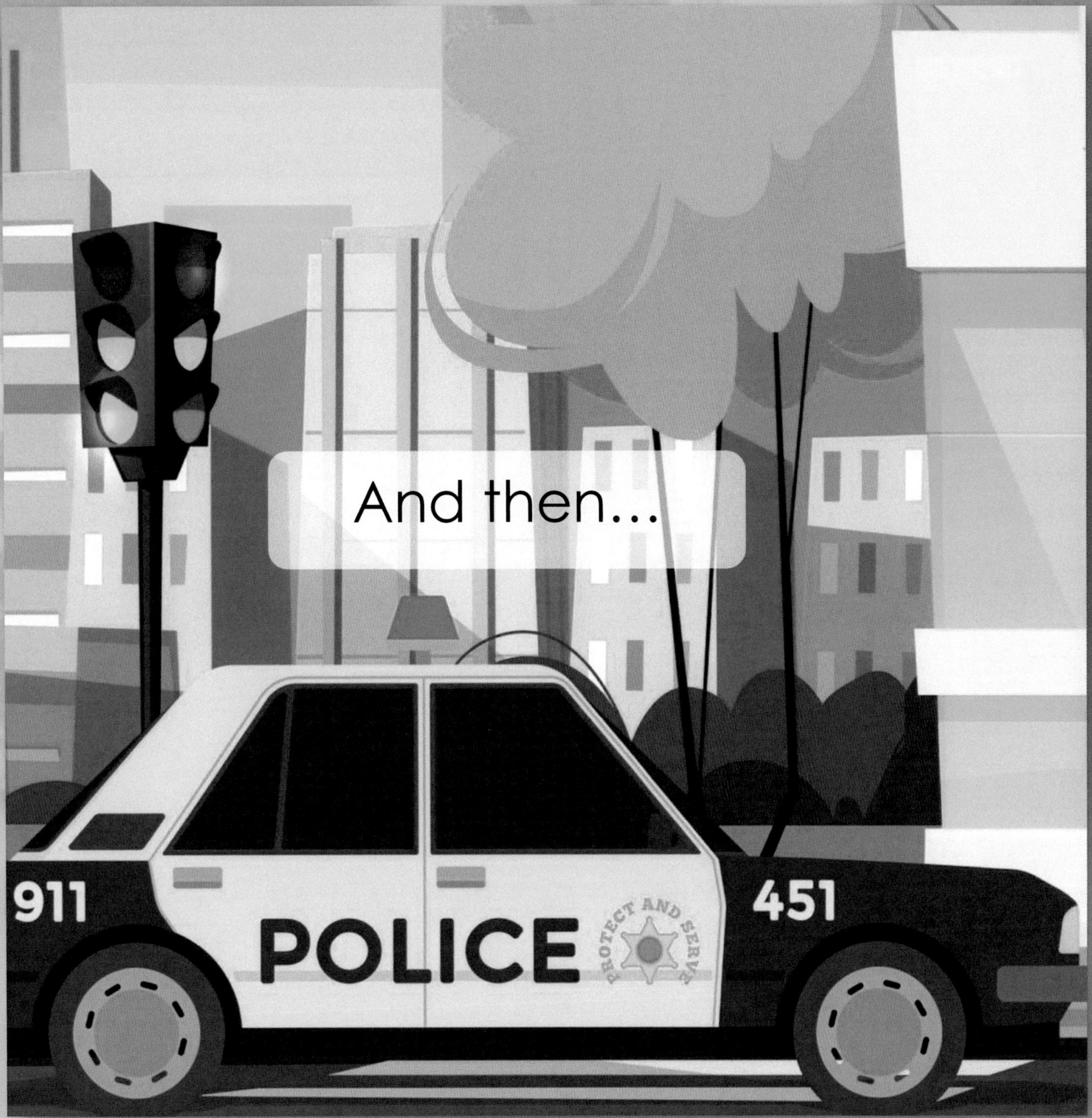

And then...

The next shift arrives,

STATION
and they were back to TEN!

POLICE
KIDS BOOKS

Made in the USA
Middletown, DE
05 October 2023